Breaking Sin

Renee,
Thanks for reading!

Chapter One

"Hold it! Please hold the elevator!" I yelled as I ran across the lobby as the elevator doors began to close. I was running late for my first class of the day. The man inside reached out and stuck his hand between the closing doors causing them to spring back open. "Thanks" I muttered, out of breath, smiling at him politely. His lips turned up slightly in a grin but he did not respond. I looked him out of the corner of my eye as we road down several floors in silence. His hair was dark and disheveled, and tattoos ran out from under his t-shirt sleeves. His eyes were impossibly green and I could not look away. As the bell dung and the doors popped open two campus security guards stood on the other side. The handsome person bolted through them, knocking one to the ground. I pressed my hands against the back wall of the elevator car trying to figure out what had just happened. The one guard pulled the other to his feet and they gave chase, screaming after him to stop.

I made my way to class unable to stop thinking about those blazing green eyes. My phone rang as I reached the doors to History.

"Did you hear what happened in the dorm this morning?" Taylor asked, sounding incredibly enthusiastic.

"What do you mean?" I asked backing away from the entrance as people milled through the doors.

"Some guy got in a fight and beat the shit out of like three people. Everyone around campus is talking about it." She was entirely too excited. My mind went back to the stranger in the elevator and my heart began to beat faster.

"I haven't talked to anyone. I stayed up studying until 3 a.m. for that bio quiz." I could almost hear her rolling her eyes.

"Before college is over we need to get you a life. You're missing out on the best parts!"

"We've talked about this." I said, pulling open the doors to the classroom and making my way to my seat. "I have to go."

"Wait! There is a dollar beer night tonight at Filly's."

"Not a chance" I rolled my eyes and flipped through my notes from last night.

"Just think about it."

"I'll consider it." I rolled my eyes again and hung the phone up before she could go on. I had absolutely no intention of going out with her tonight. I needed every waking moment I could spare to catch up on work I had missed while visiting back home. My mother had had a cancer scare and I spent several weeks with her helping her sort out the ordeal. We were all each other had in this world and when she needed me, I dropped everything to be by her side. It was the scariest time of my life.

By the time I had finished my last class I was barely hanging on to consciousness. I made my way back to my room. I lay across my bed and pulled out my notes from today. My phone lit up and I slid it under my pillow.

"Not now" I said under my breath as I flipped through the pages.

"Sinthia I can hear your phone from out here!" Taylor yelled from the other side of my dorm room door. I had met Taylor during freshman orientation. She and I were polar opposites. Her hair was dirty blonde and wildly curly, she cursed like a sailor and every boy in the school fawned over her like helpless puppies. For some reason she was determined to drag me along to every adventure college had to offer.

"Shit" I muttered under my breath and got up to answer it. She stood with her hands on her hips, tapping her foot.

"You've been avoiding my calls." Her eyes narrowed as she crossed her arms over her chest. I rolled my eyes and walked back to my bed.

"I have to study."

"You have to take a break before you wither up and die in this god forsaken place."

"That's dramatic," I said dryly.

"One drink, I'm not asking you to burn bibles in the middle of campus. Just have some fun for once." She waited for me to answer. I knew she was right. She just wanted me to have the full college experience before going out into the world and settling down. My life had been perfectly planned out in my head since I was sixteen. I would meet a man who was work driven and kind, have two children and raise our family in a quiet suburb somewhere on the east coast. My mother would come and live with us, serving as a babysitter and of course, my best friend.

"One drink?" I asked over the rim of my dark glasses.

"Yes!" She squealed hugging me enthusiastically. She held me back at arm's length and looked me over. "We have to do something about your hair first." She said with mock-disgust. I smacked her playfully on the arm, tugging the hair-tie from my hair, letting long brown tendrils cascade down my back. I did my best to stick my chest out, mocking her playfully.

"Better?" I asked, waiting for her approval.

"Getting there" she nodded with a playful grin. I grabbed a small mirror and put on some mascara and lip-gloss. By the time we left the sun was just beginning to set.

Filly's Bar overflowed with college students out for a good time and a cheap price. I tugged at my tank top, wishing I had changed before coming out, not that anyone would notice me next to Taylor. The girls around me wore short skirts and tops that barely contained them. I made a face at Taylor, pleading with her silently to take me home.

"You look fine." Taylor said, grabbing my glasses from my face and shoving them into her purse. I tried to protest but she held up her hand to stop me. "I'll give them back I promise. Let everyone see your green eyes. They're so pretty!" My mind flashed to the boy in the elevator. My green eyes did not hold a candle to his.

We made our way through the cramped dance floor to the bar. Taylor had to shout over the music to order us drinks. She turned around, handing me a beer as we studied the people around us. "It's not so bad." she shouted. I took a long swig from my beer bottle and nodded.

"Could be worse but I guess that depends on your definition of bad." I agreed, and she smiled triumphantly. I drank another large sip, holding up my bottle and peering inside. "Almost time to go." I warned, and drank the last few sips of my beer. She frowned and turned back to the bar.

"Two more beers and two shots of vodka!" She yelled to the bartender. I glared at her, slamming my bottle down on the bar. "Live a little" she said, holding up a shot glass for me to take. I drank it down, the harsh liquid burning my throat. I quickly slammed back my beer, trying to soothe it. "Let's mingle" She grabbed my arm and pulled me away from the bar. I pulled back against her, but she tugged harder.

"I don't know anybody here." I protested.

"Exactly my point!" She called back at me as she made her way into a circle of people. She let go of my arm and I rubbed my wrist. They greeted each other, giving hugs as I slinked into the background. I sipped at my beer slowly, taking in the scene. A group of girls hollered from the doorway as three guys walked in. They laughed and made their way straight to the bar. The first was smaller, with sandy blonde hair, followed by a much larger man with the same color hair. They could have been brothers. The third had dark, messy hair with tattoos scattered over his arms. I recognized him immediately from the elevator.

"Taylor" I called, trying to get her attention, but she had her arms wrapped around some burley guy's neck and he was whispering into her ear. The green-eyed hottie glanced my way, a hint of a smile on his lips and I looked down at my feet, blushing.

"Can you grab us some drinks?" Taylor yelled over the music. I nodded and made my way to the opposite side of the bar, trying not to look over at the group of guys that were now surrounded by woman.

I held up my fingers to the bartender, signaling for two more drinks. He opened them and sat them on the bar in from of me. I pulled out some cash and set it on the bar, making my way back though the crowd.

"Thanks Sinthia!" Taylor hugged my neck tightly, already half-tipsy.

"I think that guy over there is the one that got in that fight at me dorm." I yelled in her ear. She looked around at the bar.

"That guy?" she asked. "That's Collin. He's got one hell of a reputation." She laughed as the man she had been hanging on all night came up behind her, wrapping his arms around her waist.

"That's saying a lot coming from you." I joked and she scowled at me. Her attention quickly turned back to the stranger that was now nibbling on her earlobe and whispering to her. She giggled over enthusiastically and I rolled my eyes. I wished I had stayed home to study.

The night dragged on and after a few more drinks, I had loosened up enough to join in on some of the conversation, which mostly consisted of clothing and random hookups. Eventually, I had found my way to the dance floor.

"This is so much fun!" Taylor screamed and I could not hold back my laughter.

"It's not so bad. I mean, it is slightly more tolerable than say…water boarding." I shrugged, trying to move my hips to the rhythm. I am sure I looked like I was having some sort of seizure next to Taylor, but thanks to the alcohol coursing through my veins I did not care. I spun around, putting my back against her as we moved our hips together. I glanced over at the bar and my eyes locked on to Collin. I bit my lip tucking my hair behind my ear. He grinned back at me, oblivious to the girl that was whispering in his ear and rubbing her hand across his chest.

Suddenly, the wind escaped my lungs as I was shoved forcefully across the floor. Two guys had begun arguing and the one pushed the other, sending him flying directly into me. My drink spilled all over the front of my shirt, completely soaking me. "What the fuck!"

"Holy shit, Sinthia! Are you okay?" Taylor asked. Out of nowhere, Collin was on the other side of me. He grabbed the man who had pushed the other guy his collar. Holding him back at arm's length, he swung full force. His fist collided with the guy's jaw, sending him falling to the dance floor. Collin did not let up; he stood over him, hitting him repeatedly. The guy begged him to stop, holding up his arms to protect himself. Others around him joined in and the room was suddenly chaos.

"Let's go!" Taylor yelled, grabbing my arm and pulling me out of the way. The crowd was pushing all around us. Some were trying to escape while others wanting a better view of the fight or trying to get in on the action. Taylor's hand lost its gripped and soon a few people stood between us.

"Taylor!" I yelled over the music and the screaming of the crowd. Collin looked back at me and I stared at him, unable to move.

The front doors pushed open and someone yelled that the cops where here. The room erupted in panic as people hurried to leave.

"Taylor!" I screamed again as the crowd moved her further and further from me. The guy she had been hanging out with all night pulled her towards the exit, as I stood frozen.

"Let's go" Collin said, as he wrapped his arm around my waist and pulled me towards the back of the bar, away from the main exit. I searched the crowd but Taylor was no longer around. We pushed through a door labeled 'employees only'. After we snaked through a small corridor, we were outside in the cool night air.

Collin nodded to the two guys he had come in with who sat in a small black SUV. The back door flew open and I panicked, not sure if I was being saved or kidnapped. I pulled back from him. He looked down at me, his face twisted in confusion then changed to what seemed to be amusement.

"I'm not going to hurt you. Come on." He said, pulling me towards the car with a smirk on his face. I bit my lip and reluctantly slid into the backseat as more people filed out of the bar and ran in every direction. Collin slid in beside me and tapped the seat in front of him. "Let's go!" The car took off in the darkness with no headlights on to guide the way. I grabbed at my seatbelt but I panicked, pulling it too hard, causing it to lock in place.

"Calm down" he said quietly as he reached across me and tugged gently on the strap, and locked it into place. His close proximity made my heart skip a beat. His friends hollered and laughed as we made our way towards campus, but I felt like I was going to be sick.

"Pull over" I said, but my voice barely came out. "Pull over!" I shouted a little louder. The laughter dulled down and the vehicle pulled off to the side off the road. "I can find my way from here." I said, trying not to sound ungrateful. I unbuckled my seatbelt and opened the door. The night air was cool and I instantly felt better on solid ground.

"Wait" Collin called after me, and opened his door. We walked over to me and I took a step back, not sure what his intentions were. He laughed to himself. "Go ahead guys. I'll catch up with you later." He said to the driver, nodding his head. The car took off into the darkness, leaving me standing, alone, with Collin.

"What's your name?" he asked, a boyish grin creeping across his face.

"Sinthia" I said quietly, tucking my hair behind my ear.

"Sin? That is badass. My names Collin."

"I know." I replied, regretting the words as soon as they left my mouth. His grin grew larger across his face as he ran his hands through his dark hair.

"No wonder you look so scared." He joked, but I did not relax.

"Decker Hall, right? I'll walk you home. Never know who you might run into out here." He winked and my stomach tied in knots.

"I can manage. Thanks for the ride." I turned away from him and began to walk down the alley, not sure where I was, but I needed to get away from him. He was everything I did not want in a guy and I was finding it hard not to twirl my hair like an idiot and giggle at his every word. He jogged up next to me, grabbing my arm. I held my breath, afraid of what he was going to do. He released my arm when he saw my expression, taking a step back.

"I was just going to show you a shortcut." He explained, gesturing to the houses beside us. I nodded and reluctantly stepped forward. He grabbed my hand, lacing his fingers in mine and pulled me behind him.

"You are very different from the other girls at the bar." He said offhandedly and I recoiled, feeling like he was making fun of me. He pulled my hand back closer to him as we walked through the next row of houses.

"I didn't mean it like that." He ran his free hand through his messy hair. "Most girls at that bar don't try so desperately to get away from me." His eyes flashed to mine and I felt my cheeks burn pink. I looked to the ground trying hard not to show him how much he affected me.

"I'm immune to bullshit." I shot back, rolling my eyes. The alcohol was making me a little too honest. He laughed and I could not help but smile at him.

I could see my dorm across the parking lot and he stopped to face me.

"It's been fun."

"Thanks for walking me home and for...everything else." I pulled my fingers from his and began walking towards the building.

"Hey!" He called after me. "You want to hang?" He stared at me expectantly.

"I should really get some sleep. " I said, shaking my head.

"Yea, me too I guess. It was nice meeting you, Sin." He smiled and I felt my face light up.

"Yea, it was definitely a night to remember." I replied and he looked down to the ground, kicking around some stones. "If you want...maybe we can get a drink or something?" I could not stop myself. He had just defended my honor in front of a crowd of people. The least I could do was buy him a drink.

"Cool." We walked across the parking lot and I was glad it was dark so he could not see the stupid grin that was plastered across my face.

"So, you don't live on campus?" I asked, trying to make small talk.

"No, my friends and I rent an apartment down on Sicily Street." He explained. We made our way past the building and to a little dive bar on the other side of the main road. The place was practically empty, aside from a handful of locals. Collin ordered us two beers and I pulled money out of my pocket to cover it. "What are you doing?" He asked, looking genuinely offended.

"I owe you a drink." I shrugged and sat the money on the bar. He rolled his eyes and held out the beers.

"Can you hold these for a moment?" he asked.

"Sure." I took the drinks from him as he turned back to the bar. He pulled money from his wallet and set it down. He grabbed my bill and stuck it down the front of my tank top. I was unable to stop him with the beers in my hands. I glared at him, struggling to keep from laughing.

"Now you owe me a lap dance." He laughed.

"I could always pour this beer on you."

"Is that how your shirt got all wet like that?" He teased.

"Shit" I muttered looking down at my still damp shirt. I wished I had stopped at my room to change into something else before going out again. He leaned in closer, taking his drink from my hand.

"You look beautiful." He whispered into my ear, sending a jolt of happiness through my body. I stepped back from him, hating how impossible he was to ignore.

"You play?" I asked, looking at the lone pool table in the back of the room.

"Do I play?" he replied sarcastically. I rolled my eyes and made my way to the table, pulling out the balls to rack. I went first, since Collin was convinced that I would miss everything on the table. I drew back and shot, nailing the cue ball hard and sending it spinning down the table, sinking three balls. He looked shocked as I hit another in. On my next shot, I missed as I watched him staring at a group of girls who had wandered in and sat down at a table across from us.

"Your turn" I said quietly as I leaned on my pool stick and drank down the rest of my beer. He leaned over and hit the ball, completely missing his target." I thought you said you played?" I teased.

"I didn't say I played well." He joked, finishing his beer.

"I'll grab us a couple more." I walked over to the bar and waited for the bartender to come my way. As I waited I noticed one of the girls from the table leave her seat, glancing in my direction as she made a beeline for Collin. She touched his arm as she flirted with him and they talked. She giggled entirely too loudly as he smiled at her, leaning back onto the table. "Two beers" I said to the bartender who stood behind me. I placed my money on the bar and made my way back to Collin who was slipping a piece of paper into his pocket that the girl had given him before making her way back to her friends. I did my best to smile and look un-phased by the exchange.

"Thanks" He said, grabbing the beer and taking a drink.

"Making friends?" I gestured to the girls as I took a drink.

"I'm a people person." He smiled and I rolled my eyes, lining up my next shot. We played several more games until the bar emptied out and the bartender yelled for last call. After we had finished our drinks, we walked back across the parking lot towards my dorm.

"I had a lot of fun tonight." Collin smiled.

"Yea, I did too, surprisingly." I replied.

"Ouch" He put his hand on his chest, pretending to be wounded.

"No, I didn't mean it that way. I just don't go out very often and I didn't expect to enjoy it as much as I did." I tucked my hair behind my ear and a piece fell loose in front of my face. Collin reached out and tucked it back, his fingers running along my cheek. "I should probably go." I said nervously. He nodded letting his hand drop to his side.

"See you around?" He asked as I walked towards the building.

"Yea" I yelled back at him.

Chapter Two

My alarm wailed above my head and I swung my arm at it, trying to shut it off. It was just out of reach and I reluctantly pushed off my bed to hit the button. My head throbbed and for a moment I was not sure I would make it to class. I got a glass of water and some aspirin and headed down to the showers, hoping it would make me feel well enough to stay awake.

My classes dragged on and by the end of the day, I could not see straight. Part of that was due to leaving my glasses in Taylor's purse. My phone rang as I made my way across campus towards the dorm.

"What did *you* do last night?" Taylor asked.

"Hello to you too" I said dryly.

"Hello. What the hell happened with you and Collin last night?" Her question caught me off guard.

"You know I didn't do anything, Tay." I rolled my eyes and pushed the button for the elevator.

"Don't give me that. He was eye fucking you all night. Then, he went all incredible Hulk on that guy."

I laughed as the doors opened. Standing in front of me was Collin. His green eyes lit up when he saw me and for a second I forgot how to breathe.

"Hello" I said quietly as I stepped inside.

"Yea, hello. We already said all that, remember?" Taylor snapped in my ear.

"Hey" Collin replied.

"Who the fuck was that? Was that...Was that Collin? You did fuck him! You slut!" Taylor giggled in my ear and my face burned red.

"I'll call you back." I ended the call and slid my phone into my pocket. He held the door to the elevator open and I waited for him to walk out but he did not so I stepped inside.

"What are you doing here?" I asked, sounding ruder than I intended.

"I was looking for you, but I didn't know which room was yours so I may have pissed off some of the people on your floor." He grinned and my heart began to speed up.

"Why?" I asked.

"I don't know. Make sure you got home okay." He ran his fingers through his hair and it fell perfectly back into place. I bit my lip. He made me incredibly nervous. Most guys did not bother to approach me. I usually kept to myself, aside from the rare occasion that I let Taylor drag me out for a drink.

"Here I am." I smiled like an idiot, than quickly erased it from my face. What the hell was this guy doing to me? Two girls filed passed him into the elevator, giggling and smiling. He grinned their direction but his eyes came quickly back to mine.

"So, I'll see you around?" He asked as he stepped out of the elevator and the girls in the corner got quiet, waiting for my response.

"I guess I will if you keep stalking me like this." I resorted to sarcasm to hide my nervousness. He laughed as the doors slid closed. I glanced back at the girls behind me who were looking me up and down as if I had an infectious disease.

I could not wait to get inside my room. As soon as I closed the door behind me, I leaned back against it. My phone rang loudly in my hand.

"What the fuck was that about?" Taylor yelled.

"It was nothing. I just ran into Collin in the elevator."

"You do know he doesn't even live in our dorm, don't you?"

"He didn't stay with me last night, Tay. He's not even my type."

"You have a type?"

"You're exhausting." I sighed, throwing my books on my bed.

"Get dressed. I'll be over in five." She said, hanging up before I could object. I lay back on my bed and stared up at the ceiling wishing it would swallow me whole.

A knock came a few minutes later and Taylor did not even bother to wait for a response. She came and plopped next to me on the bed.

"Wake up sleepy head!" She bounced the mattress and I grabbed my stomach.

"Come on, Taylor" I whined, opening my eyes to see her smiling. "Where?"

"I wanna grab some burgers at Smokey's before the rush." Smokey's was a burger joint just out on the main road. Everyone on campus hung out there.

"Fine" I pushed off the bed crossed my arms over my chest.

"That's my girl" She beamed and looped her arm in mine, pulling me up.

I picked at my burger, not really feeling well enough to eat. Taylor grilled me about my time with Collin, not believing that anyone could be alone with him and not drop their panties.

"He didn't even try, Tay." I said, trying not to sound disappointed.

"Speak of the sexy devil." She said grinning. I glanced behind me to see Collin walk through the door with his friends from the bar. I sunk lower in the booth and hoped he did not see me. I do not even know why I cared. He was good looking, sure, but he was nothing but trouble waiting to happen. I have watched Taylor enough with those kinds of guys to know it was not anything I wanted. He was a heartbreak waiting to happen and I refused to be his next victim.

"He's looking at you" Taylor gushed and I glanced to the other side of the room. Collin was staring passed the server, directly at me. I felt my cheeks begin to burn and I smiled quickly at him. He grinned and nodded once at me. I bit my lip and looked back to Taylor who was glowing. "He fucking wants you." She laughed. I rolled my eyes and looked back his way. Three girls had joined them and Collin had his arm around a girl with short blonde hair.

"I think your radar is a little off." I said, dropping a piece of my burger. She leaned in closer to me.

"You really do like him?" She said.

"Looks like everyone does" I rolled my eyes and took a long drink from my soda. "There is no way I could ever take a guy like that home to meet my mother."

"They're leaving." She said and I tried my best not to look up at him, but I gave in, glancing out of the corner of my eye.

"Sin" Collin nodded and my heart leapt into my throat. The blonde on his arm looked bored.

"Hey" I smiled politely, glancing over at Taylor. They continued out of the restaurant and I kicked Taylor under the table.

"What the fuck was that for?" She reached under the table, rubbing her shin.

"Pick a reason." I said, half joking.

"How about...the fact that we are going out tonight?" She said, pulling back so I would not hit her again.

"I can't" I shook my head as she began to nod.

"I'm sure Collin will be there." She said as if that would convince me.

"And all of the girls he is sleeping with" I joked.

"This is your chance to show him what he is missing."

"Even if he did like me, it wouldn't go anywhere."

"I know, but it's still fun to flirt." She narrowed her eyes, waiting for me to give in.

"What time?" I sighed. I hated when she begged me, I could never say no.

"Eight"

"I'm going to regret this."

Chapter Three

I never should have let Taylor dress me up. I looked like a two-bit hooker. My shirt was low cut with three buttons down the center that Taylor insisted be undone and she matched it with a short jean skirt.

"You luck fucking amazing." Taylor reassured me as we walked into Filly's. Several guys turned to look at us as we made our way to the back. "Told you" She whispered and I could not help but smile.

"Fuck" I muttered.

"What?"

"He's here." I whispered. Collin was at the bar, his back to us as we approached. I stepped behind Taylor as she ordered us a round of drinks.

"I'll get that." Collin nodded to us, putting money on the bar. The bartender nodded back at him.

"Thanks" I yelled over the music. He moved over closer to us. I stepped out from behind Taylor and his eyes looked me up and down.

"Wow, Sin. You clean up nice." He smiled and I had to look away. After a moment of awkward silence, I tried to make some casual conversation.

"Where's your girlfriend?"

"What?" He signaled that he could not hear me. I leaned in closer.

"Your girlfriend?" I said louder, enunciating each word.

"You want to be my girlfriend? I'm flattered." He said, pulling back and placing his hand on his chest.

"No" I smacked his arm and he rubbed in in mock pain. I was surprised at how hard his muscles were. He laughed and leaned back in closer. I could feel his warn breath on my neck and it sent goose bumps down my back.

"Too bad" he replied and my breath hitched in my throat. His face lingered next to mine for a moment.

"I hope I'm not interrupting." The girl he had been with at the Smokey's said as she smiled at us.

"Not at all." He smiled and pulled back from me. She wrapped her arms around his waist. I took a long drink from my beer and turned around searching for Taylor. I spotted her a few feet away doing shots with a bunch of frat boys.

"I'll see you later." I said, wanting more than anything to get away from the awkward situation.

"I hope so." He replied, his green eyes smoldering. The blonde was nuzzling her face into his neck but he seemed oblivious.

I found my way back over to Taylor.

"Can we go?" I asked as she slammed back a shot.

"One more drink?" She stuck out her lower lip. I grabbed the shot glass in front of her and slammed it back.

"Can we go now?" She rolled her eyes at me.

"What happened with Collin?"

I pointed back behind me and she made a face of disgust.

"What a whore! Let's show him what he is missing!" She said and she grabbed my arm, pulling me back to the dance floor.

"Oh, no! Remember what happened last night?" I begged.

"I remember someone coming to defend your honor." She smirked and I did not have a response.

We danced the night away into the early morning hours. When I could barely stand any longer, I begged Taylor to take me home.

"I'm not ready to go yet!" She whined.

"I'll take you." Collin's voice said in my ear. I turned around to see him standing, alone.

I stuttered trying to come up with a witty response.

"That is a great idea." Taylor said with laughter in her voice. I glared at her as my ears burned and I could feel myself beginning to flush. Before I could protest, he laced his fingers in mine and pulled me closer. I put my other hand on his back as he led me through the crowd of people. His muscles flexed under my fingers.

The cool air of the outside was refreshing. I took a deep breath, happy to be out of the smoke filled building. He nodded to his friend's across the parking lot and we walked quickly to the dark SUV.

"Want to go to my place?" he asked, his lips curled up in a smile.

"I'm not going to fuck you." I rolled my eyes and pulled my hand back, but he squeezed it tighter.

"I didn't ask." He smirked and I felt humiliated. "I know you're not like that." He added. I relaxed when I realized he was not expecting anything from me. As good looking as he was I did not want to be anything more than friends.

"Let's go" I said, thankful for the alcohol that gave me courage. We slid into the dark car and pulled off into the night. Collin stared out the window as his thumb gently brushed against my knuckles. I was not sure why he was still holding my hand but I did not complain. It was comforting. I tugged at my skirt wishing I had not let Taylor dress me. I glanced over at Collin whose eyes were on my legs. He quickly looked away, grinning.

"So, what happened to the blonde?" I asked, trying to fill the awkward silence.

"Which one" His friend laughed from the front seat.

"She became increasingly more annoying the drunker she got." He explained.

"How sad" I muttered under my breath. He laughed quietly. Collin was not as bad a person as I made him out to be. Sure, he was a womanizer, but as a friend, he was very easy to get along with and he looked out for me, which was sweet.

We pulled up to an apartment building just off campus. Collin slid out of the car and stood by the door waiting for me. I got out of the car as gracefully as I could in the ridiculous outfit. We walked, hand in hand to the door. As he pushed it open, I sighed at the giant set of stairs ahead of me. I slipped off my heels and followed behind him.

The apartment was nice. It had minimal furniture but was clean with an open floor plan, which made it feel larger than it actually was.

"You want a drink?" he asked as he walked into the kitchen and grabbed a bottle from above the fridge.

"Sure" I said, looking around. "You play?" I asked looking down at the video game system hooked up to the large flat screen television.

"Do I play?" He scoffed and drank back his shot. I walked over to the counter and took my shot, slamming it back. It burned but I had had enough that it did not bother me anymore.

"Want to play with me?" I asked. He smiled and poured another round for us.

"Of course I'd like to play with you." He winked and I wanted to reach across the counter and smack him.

"Bye" I said and turned towards the door. He hurried around the counter and grabbed my arm.

"I'm sorry. I can't help it." He laughed. I rolled my eyes and went back to the counter to drink my shot.

"Yea, we can play. Let me change first. You want something to wear?" he asked and I bit my lip wondering if I should. "You can't kill zombies in an outfit like that." He joked and headed back the hallway. I followed behind him as he dug through his closet for something to wear. He pulled out a white t-shirt and tossed it at me. I looked around for somewhere to change. "I won't look." He said. His back was to me as he pulled off his shirt. It was wide and muscular and covered in tattoos. He slid off his jeans and put on a pair of basketball shorts. I bit my lip as I slinked out of my clothing and pulled the shirt over my head. He grabbed a pair of boxers from his drawer and handed them to me.

"You said you wouldn't look." He rolled his eyes and turned back around. I pulled them on quickly and headed back into the living room.

We played for hours until the sun began to shine through the windows. We polished off his bottle of liquor and both of us could barely keep our eyes open.

"I think I should go." I yawned. He rubbed his eyes, blinking to keep them open.

"I'm too tired to take you home."

"That's okay. I can walk." I got up from the couch and stretched.

"No. Just stay. You can sleep in my bed." He stood up in front of me.

"Fine" I was too exhausted to protest. We grabbed my hand and I followed him back the hallway to his room. I stared at the bed as he pulled down the blankets and slipped under them. I had assumed he would sleep somewhere else, like the couch. I wanted to say something but it would have been rude to kick him out of his own bed.

"Can you get the light?" He asked, yawning. I flicked off the switched and cursed at myself under my breath as I slid under the covers next to him. I scooted as close to the edge as possible. His breathing became deeper and I relaxed knowing he had fallen asleep.

I awoke the next day at around three in the afternoon. The sun was shining brightly through the windows and it took me a moment to place where I was. The bed was empty and I sat up, stretching. I heard some shuffling down the hall so I walked out to find where Collin had gone.

"It's kind of late for a walk of shame." The shorter blonde guy said from the fridge.

"It's not like that." I said under my breath. He looked back at me smiling.

"Don't be a dick." Collin called from behind me. He has just gotten out of the shower and he was only wearing a towel wrapped loosely around his waist. My eyes immediately were drawn to the wonderful v-shaped muscles that let down below the towel's edge. "Hungry?" Collin asked, and I realized I had been staring at him like an idiot.

"Yea" I stuttered.

"Jake this is Sin." He motioned back to me as he dug through the fridge. Jake glanced back it me with a half-cocked smile.

"Sin?" he laughed. "Ahhh... You're a stripper!" He yelled.

"You really are a dick." I snapped back. Collin stood up straight and was glaring over at his roommate with an angry scowl.

"Just a joke guys" He stammered and walked out of the kitchen. Collin's gaze turned to me and the corner of his mouth turned up in a proud smile.

"You just officially replaced Jake as my best friend."

Chapter Four

Several weeks had passed since I had met Collin. We spent nearly every night together out at the local bars with Taylor, Jake and Beef. Beef was Collin's taller blonde roommate. I had no idea what his real name was but I felt like an absolute fool calling him Beef. I giggled like a twelve year old every time it left my lips, especially if I had been drinking.

"Beeeeef!" I yelled down the bar, laughing my ass off.

"How are you going to be an effective wingman if you are falling down drunk?" Beef asked with a grin on his face. He hung his arm over my shoulder.

"So tell me, is Beef a family name?" I laughed again and he squeezed my neck with his arm playfully. Sometimes I think he forgot that I was a girl. "Oww!" I yelped and he immediately released.

"What the fuck?" Collin asked, putting his arm over my shoulder protectively. I laughed thinking in my head about Beef's father having the same name. Would that make him Beef Junior. I do not know why this was so funny, but I doubled over, laughing so hard no sound actually came out.

"That's nice. You let her get wasted? How is she supposed to be wingman if she's wasted?" Collin scolded Beef.

"I'm fine." I said shooting back up to a standing position, flinging my hair in Collin's face. "Pick" I said, trying to decide which blurry image of Collin to look at. He rolled his eyes and shifted his weight on his feet. "Fucking pick." He scanned the bar for woman.

"That one" he pointed to a petite brunette that had golden streaks running through her hair.

"Ugghh...really?" I asked. Looking at him with my face screwed tight. He sighed loudly like a child who had just been told they could not have their favorite toy. "Alright, alright. Calm down." I slinked out from under Collin's arm and staggered my way down the bar. "Beer" I called to the bartender who gave me a sideways grin but set the bottle on the bar. I should have been cut off hours ago but

Collin was good friends with the owner. I grabbed my beer and spun around.

"God he's fucking hot." I muttered. The brunette next to me looked my way, then her eyes drifted passed me. "He has been eye fucking you all damn night."

"Me?" She asked, surprised. I looked the other way and rolled my eyes.

"Yea. I tried to dance with him earlier but he just pushed me away."

"He pushed you?" Her eyes narrowed and I realized I had said something wrong.

"No, no. Not like, literally. He has been turning down girls left and right. Honestly, I'm so fucking jealous of you right now." I turned my head away again and pretended to gag. I saw Collin's eyes light up as if he was holding back laughter.

"I'm going to go talk to him." She said, pulling her top down and making sure your boobs were practically falling out of her shirt. "Thanks" She winked at me and I winked back, turning around to the bar.

"Wingman?" The guy next to me asked. He had a few tattoos scattered down his arms and his hair was a sandy color. Overall, he was decent looking but nothing about him particularly stood out.

"Yup" I replied, sipping on my beer

"Me too." He turned around to face the floor and I followed suit. "My guys over there." He gestured with his head to a guy across the room will black hair that hung down to his ears.

"That's my guy." I nodded in the direction of Collin.

"Uh oh" He said quietly.

"What?" I asked.

"Does he know that you're in love with him?" he joked. I playfully hit him on the arm.

"It's not like that." I said, rolling my eyes and taking a long drink from my bottle. I finished it and turned back around to the bar, waiting for the bartender to get me another.

"So you're single?" he asked, a grin spread across his face.

"Hey Sin, how you feeling?" Beef placed his hand protectively on the small of my back.

"Like a rock star." I slurred. "Beef, I think the bartender is ignoring me."

"You are probably right." He cleared his throat and pushed himself between my new friend and me. "Collin wants me to take you home." He said, bracing for an argument. I glanced down the bar at Collin. He was making out with the little brunette and oblivious to anything around him.

"No way. Where's Taylor?" I asked, scanning the floor. I found her grinding on the dance floor with a person I had set her up with hours ago.

"She wants to stay. I can take her home." New friend said from behind Beef. I nodded and held up my beer while Beef turned around and glared at him. He took his drink and headed out onto the dance floor.

"Fuck, Beef. Why did you do that?" I whined.

"You never would have gone home with him anyway. You never do." He answered holding up two fingers to the bartender. She gave Beef a hard stare but set the bottles in front of us.

"Finally" I sighed, grabbing the bottle and taking a long drink. Beef looked at me sideways and shook his head.

"When I first met you we could barely get you to have two drinks. Now you drink more than all of us combined." I did not respond. I liked being more outgoing, having more friends, people who wanted to spend time with me.

"Let's go," I said, sitting my bottle on the bar behind me. Beef nodded and looped his arm in mine, weaving me through the crowd.

I crawled under the covers in Collin's bed. The room spun around me and I grabbed at the covers trying to make the world stand still.

A few hours later, I awoke to the sound of Collin banging into the bedroom door and the tripping over his own feet as he pulled off his shoes and threw them on the floor.

"Fuck" I yelled throwing my pillow at him.

"Sorry" he mumbled and crawled under the covers next to me.

"Have fun?" I asked.

"Same as usual" He said.

"Man-whore" I joked.

"Prude" I could hear the smile in his voice.

The next day I managed to take myself to most of my classes. At lunch, we all met at Smokey's for burgers and laughed about our fun from the night before.

"Here is to Sin! For being the best wingman this group could hope for!" Jake said, holding up his beer. I held up my diet coke, clinking it against his bottle as I adjusted my sunglasses.

"Fuck. It is so bright." I mumbled. Collin put his arm around me and pulled me close to him.

"How about tonight we order in? Let our little matchmaker have a break." He said kissing the top of my head.

"I'm supposed to meet that Derek guy again tonight!" Taylor protested.

"I'm fine." I said, waving away their worries.

"How about tonight we find someone for our little Sin to take home." Jake suggested playfully.

"No" I waved my hands again. Taylor snorted and the boys all turned their heads in her direction.

"What?" Collin asked as she drank from her cup, not meeting any of their eyes.

"She's just not like us." She finally answered.

"What? She doesn't hook up?" Jake joked. Taylor took another sip from her soda as their eyes slowly went from her to me. I sank down lower in my seat.

"Sin, are you...a lesbian?" I threw a French fry at his face.

"No, Dick" I scoffed at him. They all began to laugh and joke around me but Collin stayed quiet, his arm wrapped tightly around me. It was not that I was against hooking up with someone, I just had a certain type that I was looking for and that kind of person did not hang out at Filly's until all hours of the night.

Chapter Five

I stayed home with Collin playing video games while the rest of the group went down to the bar. We drank a few shots but kept it mild in comparison to the nights we spent out. We ordered Chinese food and as the night went on, we cuddle up on the couch watching a scary movie. Every time I jumped, he would laugh and make fun of me for being such a girl.

He poured us a few more shots and by the time the movie was over, I was ready for bed. We made our way back to Collin's bedroom and settled in for the night.

"Collin?" I asked in the dark, hoping he was still awake.

"Yea, Sin?" He yawned as he said my name. I curled up tighter in the covers.

"Don't fucking laugh at me, okay?" I waited for him to agree.

"Okay"

"I'm scared." I waited for his response. He did not say a word. He slowly slid himself closer and wrapped his arms around my waist, pulling my tightly against him. I could feel his hard chest muscles against my back. I felt safe. I closed my eyes.

"Sin?" he asked.

"Yea?"

"What did Taylor mean with that whole thing at Smokey's?" I held my breath trying to decide how to respond.

"What thing?" I asked, my voice small.

"I know you don't hook up with people at the bar. I get that. But..." His voice trailed off and his body tensed behind me.

"What?" I asked, my voice shaking.

"Are you..." His voice trailed off again as he struggled to find the right words.

"I'm not a lesbian." I said dryly. He chuckled, his hot breath on the back of my neck.

"I know. I just…never mind." He snuggled in closer to me. I breathed out a deep sigh and closed my eyes.

The next day the sun burned through the windows. I tried to get off the bed but Collin's arms squeezed tighter around me.

"Collin." I tried to wake him.

"No" he responded, his grip not loosening. I pulled against him again.

"Collin." I said a little louder.

Shh…." He responded, his hands circling my body and pulling me firmly against him. His breath was blowing hot into my ear. I wriggled against him again and his hips grinded into me.

"Seriously?" I yelled as I grabbed his hands and pried them off me. He rolled over, rubbing his eyes.

"What?" he asked, his arms outstretched.

"Nothing" I sighed and stalked off to the bathroom. I jumped in the shower and washed away the smell of stale cigarette smoke and liquor. The door opened and closed and I stood frozen behind the thin curtain.

"Collin?" I asked, afraid of what voice would answer.

"Yea?" He replied as he turned on the sink.

"Do you mind?"

"Not at all." He responded as he continued to brush his teeth. After a few moments of standing completely naked and still just inches from him the door to the bathroom opened and closed again as he left. I quickly washed my hair and got dressed.

I made my way to the kitchen to cook everyone breakfast. I do not know how they ever ate before I showed up. I fried up some bacon in a pan as I prepared a large bowl of eggs to scramble. Slowly, everyone filed out into the living room.

"That smells fucking amazing!" Taylor said, stretching as she came down the hall and looking for something to eat while she waited.

"Get out of the kitchen!" I held up the spatula in a threatening manner.

"I'd listen to her, Tay! She smacked me good with that thing once. I still can't eat without having flashbacks!" Beef joked from the couch. Collin wandered down the hall, rubbing the sleep from his eyes.

"Hungry?" I asked over my shoulder.

"It's so early!" He complained, still half asleep.

"It's one o'clock in the afternoon on a Saturday." I rolled my eyes and went back to cooking. He came into the kitchen and grabbed my shoulders from behind, kissing me on the back of the head.

"Smells amazing" He whispered and went to take his place on the couch with all of the others.

We ate our food as we discussed our plans for the weekend. Everyone agreed we should make a trip into the city and try our luck at the larger clubs. As soon as we finished eating Taylor and I went off to find something to wear for tonight. We kept most of our things in the spare room at the end of the hall. We still kept our residence in the dorm, but it was just easier to crash here at the end of a long night of partying. The room had a large bed, but Taylor usually occupied it with her romantic encounters. Collin never brought anyone home, saying it is never wise to 'shit where you eat', so it was always safe to sleep in his room with him.

"Elixir is packed!" I stared out the window like a small child, dazzled by all the lights. The line curved out of the door and onto the street.

"No big deal. We can get in." Collin replied and scooted me closer to him. I smiled at him, excited to party in the big city.

We walked straight to the front door. Collin and the bouncer exchanged a few words and he unclipped the velvet rope, letting us pass through.

We made our way to the bar, ordering a round of shots for all of us.

"Here's to Sin! I am not worried about getting into Heaven 'because I'm already here!" Beef toasted, holding up his glass.

"I'll find you someone real special tonight!" I replied and gave him a grateful smile. We ordered another round to get us warmed up and I began my mission to find everyone someone to hook up with. I saved Collin for last. He looked around, unimpressed with the selection.

"Let's dance." He said as he grabbed my arm and pulled me onto the floor. I gave him a wicked grin and followed behind, ready to have a good time. I put my hands on his muscular chest as I grinding my hips into his. One song led to another and soon we were covered in sweat as we moved along with the music, our faces dangerously close.

"Mind if I cut in?" A girl asked, tapping me on the shoulder.

"Go ahead" I winked at Collin and he slowly unwrapped his arms from around me.

As the night drug on I found myself sitting at the bar, alone. This was usually how our nights out went but tonight it was especially lonely.

"Wanna dance?" I deep voice whispered in my ear. I turned around to see a strikingly handsome man in a dark button up shirt. His dark hair was cut short and he looked like he belonged on a yacht in the middle of the ocean. He definitely fit the criteria for future husband material.

"Why not" I replied, putting my hand in his and letting him lead me onto the floor. We danced for what seemed like an eternity. It was tame in comparison to the way Collin and I danced, but I was not complaining. I had my eyes closed; slowly swaying my hips to the music, wishing it would never end.

"We need to go." Collin said into my ear, pulling me from the moment.

"No way." I flipped around and laced my fingers behind my partner's neck.

"Come on" Collin's jaw was clenched and he grabbed my arm.

"What the fuck, man?" The guy said to Collin, pushing his hand off my arm.

I Held my breath waiting for Collin to react. In a split second, he pulled me off him and his arm swung back in rage. His fist connected, sending blood spraying across my chest as my partner hit the ground. The crowd formed a circle around us.

"Collin!" I screamed as he bent over, pummeling the man as he lay helpless. "Collin!" I screamed again, grabbing his arm, trying to stop his assault. After one last blow, he regained his composure, holding out his hand for me to take it. I shoved by him, hitting him hard with my shoulder as I walked out of the front door.

Chapter Six

The car was silent on the way home. Collin pulled me closer to him but I would scoot away as soon as he did.

"I'm sorry" He whispered in my ear. I pushed him away and looked out the window. He took his hand and wrapped his fingers in mine. His knuckles were bloody and swollen.

We made it to the house without fighting. I stalked off to Collin's bedroom and slammed the door behind me.

"Sin?' he knocked on the door, waiting for a response.

"It's your room. You don't have to knock." I yelled, wiping the tears from my cheeks. He came in as I pulled off my dress, ruined by the splatters of blood. I turned my back to him as I unsnapped my bra and slid it down my arms. I grabbed a tank top from the dresser and pulled it on. When I turned around to get into bed, Collin was staring at me. I glared at him and left the room, unable to look him in the eye. I made my way down the hall to the spare bedroom where Taylor and I kept our belongings. It was empty and I was grateful they decided to stay up and watch movies. I closed the door behind me and cuddled under the covers in the cold empty bed. I cried alone in the darkness for what seemed like hours as I listened to everyone laughing and having a good time in the living room.

"Sin?" Collin called from the other side of the door.

"What?" I yelled, trying to keep my voice from cracking. He opened the door and slowly made his way over to the bed. He sat down on the edge and rubbed my back softly.

"I can't sleep without you." He sounded lost and wounded. I rolled my eyes wanting to tell him that he deserved it, but I could not. I shoved off the covers and stomped passed him down the hall. Moments later, he joined me, sliding under the covers and pressing his warm body against my back. I hated how comforting it felt, even when he was the one who had upset me. I relaxed into him, curving my back against his chest. His arms gripped tightly around my waist.

"I'm sorry," He whispered in my ear, his breath tickling against my neck.

"I know" I sighed, wiping my cheek.

"I just…" His voice trailed off and I waited, hanging on his every word. "I don't want your first time to be with some random guy at the bar." My body went rigid as he spoke. I was embarrassed that he had even figured it out. His arms gripped tighter around me, pulling me into him. "I'm sorry" I did not respond. I did not know what to say. He had discovered my most intimate secret. "Look at me, please." I could hear the pleading in his voice but I was frozen.

"Sin" his breath was hot against my cheek. I slowly rolled over to face him. As I turned, his hands gripped my hips and pulled my body flush against him. I let out a heavy breath. His mouth was open and he struggled to keep his breathing even. Our lips hovered an inch from each other and I could feel how much he wanted me as his hips held firm against mine.

"Sin" his voice low.

The electricity flowed between us and I struggled to remember why I was even mad at him.

"Collin" I breathed, his name tasting sweet as it left my mouth. He pushed against me reflexively and I let out a small whimper.

"Do you have any idea how perfect you are?" His head tilted as his lips brushed against mine. I pushed my hips back against him, struggling to keep myself away. In one quick movement, he flipped me onto my back and was lying on top of me, pressing hard against my waist. He slowly moved his face closer to mine. I closed my eyes, begging for him to touch me. He froze. I opened my eyes, looking into his, searching for what I had done wrong.

"I can't" He pulled his mouth back from mine. I could not breathe. I did not even know before tonight how badly I wanted him. Had he not pulled this stunt I may have never known. He rolled off me, leaving me wide-eyed and gasping for air. I was humiliated and desperately needing him at the same time. I rolled over on my side and curled up into a ball.

After a moment, his hands slid over my waist and he pulled me back against him. I wanted so desperately to pull away from him but I could not.

Chapter Six

As the sun shined directly into my eyes, I squirmed and slid myself out of his grip. I made my way into the kitchen to get a head start on breakfast, refusing to believe last night was real. We had two eggs and no bacon left.

"Fuck" I muttered to myself as I slammed the fridge door closed. I snuck back into the bedroom and pulled on a pair of jeans. Collin was sleeping peacefully in the center of the bed.

The streets were packed for early morning and I loved the smell of fresh baked goods in the air as I made my way down the block to the market. I hardly ever seemed to make it out in the daylight hours any more. The sun felt amazing against my skin. I bought a ham steak, bacon, eggs, croissants and three different kinds of cheeses for breakfast. I blocked every awkward second of last night out of my mind as I made my way back to the apartment. I was terrified of the changes they would cause in my relationship with Collin. Somehow, I was the only person in the world he would not touch.

As I entered the apartment, Taylor jumped on me, wrapping her arms around my neck as I entered the room.

"Jesus Christ, we thought you were gone." She whispered. I stared around the room at all of my friends. Collin sat on the edge of the couch, unable to look at me.

"We needed groceries." I replied, looking at all of their faces. Taylor loosened her grip on me and turned back to the room.

"Guys? What the fuck? Do you want your eggs or not?" I joked, trying to divert attention from myself. The room erupted in cheers and I smiled, heading into the kitchen to make them all a feast worthy of kings. Taylor followed me into the kitchen, popping bread into the toaster. When the boy's conversation turned to television, she began to talk to me.

"He knows?" she asked quietly as I cracked the eggs into a large bowl. I bit my lip and nodded to her. "Did you?" she asked and I hesitated before continuing.

"No" I replied sharply, feeling uncomfortable with the discussion. It was not because I did not trust Taylor, but I was still incredibly confused with the way the night had ended. He made me feel things for him I did not know I was capable of only to turn me down. He did not want me.

Everyone ate their food ignoring the elephant in the room. I suddenly felt out of place among my friends.

"You want to go out? Maybe go to the mall?" Collin asked as everyone stared at me expectantly.

"Sure" I shrugged, looking down at my plate. Before today they all treated me like one of the guys, now I was some breakable thing.

We walked around the mall for hours.

"Sin, last night…" His voice trailed off and I could feel my cheeks burning under his stare.

"Already forgotten. I mean...we had a little too much to drink." I held my breath waiting for his reaction.

"Right" he said, rubbing the back of his neck." I just wanted to make sure you were okay." I nodded and we continued window-shopping for another hour or so before heading back to his apartment.

His entire mood had shifted. He was anxious to go out and get drunk. When he mentioned other girls, I felt a pang of jealousy but I did not let on.

The club was packed, as usual, and I took up my regular spot near the bar. After a few shots, everyone was in a great mood, even Collin. He seemed to have completely forgotten about last night and I was hoping that it meant we could go back to being the great friends we were with no weirdness. I did not factor in how my feelings for him had changed. I had always found him physically attractive but I never wanted anything more than friendship from him. I saw how he treated other girls and I did not want to be another number on a list.

Collin's eyes met mine from across the room as he danced with a red head. I turned around to face the bar, unable to watch. Everyone was laughing and having a good time and I stood alone, amongst a sea of strangers. I grabbed a shot and turned back, scanning the dance floor for Collin. I caught sight of him as he left out of the front door, his arm wrapped around the red head. He was obviously over last night.

The night dragged on and one by one, my friends left with their conquests. By four in the morning, I was barely able to stand on my own. I called a cab and had them take me back to my dorm room. I wanted to be alone. I could not stomach the thought of crawling into bed next to him after watching him with that other woman. Somehow, in the span of a day, I went from being his best friend to dying inside because we were not more.

I slept into the early evening. It was awkward waking up in my own bed and it took me a few minutes to place where I was. I grabbed my phone as I stretched, looking at my missed calls. Taylor had called me at least twenty times along with an equal amount of texts messages. I scrolled through them, worried something may have happened.

> *Where the hell are you?*

> *Did you go home with someone? You slut!*

> *Answer the phone!!!*

> *Collin is going nuts. He is worried sick about you. Please answer.*

"Shit" I mumbled as I wiped my eyes. I dialed Taylor's number. After a few rings, she picked up.

"Where the fuck are you?" She whispered into the receiver and I knew she was trying not to let Collin know I was on the phone. I heard a loud banging sound and then Collin's voice.

"Is that her? Where the fuck is she?" He was seething with anger and I could not understand why.

"Uhh...Sin? Collin is really worried." Taylor was nervous.

"I just went back to the room. I was tired." I knew it was more than that. I needed to distance myself from him. Watching him leave the club last night with his arm around someone else had really gotten to me. What did she have that I didn't? Why did I care? I had already made up my mind that he was not the right kind of person for me. If things had gone further it would have destroyed what we already have together.

"Are you coming over?" She asked and I knew she wanted me to calm Collin down, but I could not.

"I really should study. I haven't been keeping up with my work lately." I bit my lip and waited for her to say something.

"Okay" she sighed and hung up the phone. I grabbed my shower kit and headed down to the bathroom. I needed to think over the whole situation. I knew that if I spent another night lying next to Collin, things would get out of hand and I would lose him forever, because I could not have anything more with him. He was not the type to settle down and I was not looking for a relationship with someone who was incapable of giving me what I needed.

Chapter Seven

Weeks passed and I had become so good at making excuses to why I could not go out that my friends barely ever called anymore. Collin would text me when he was drunk letting me know how good of a time he was having without me. Eventually I stopped replying all together and the texts quit coming.

I had gotten my grades back up to what they were before I had started hanging out with them and it was as if none of it had ever happened. I even met a guy who had taken me out on a few dates. His hair was dark like Collin's but his eyes were a deep brown and he always had a smile on his face. Another major difference between John and Collin was I had never seen John raise a hand to anyone. He was the most caring and gentleperson I had ever met. He was everything I had ever wanted, but after spending so much time with Collin, I found myself growing bored with our game nights.

"Let's go out. I'm in the mood to have some fun." I whined and John rubbed my cheek with his fingers.

"I have a final to study for." He shook his head.

"Come on" I whined, sticking out my bottom lip for added effect.

"How about we go out to dinner?" He put his pen down on his notebook.

"Fine. How about Smokey's?" I perked up at the thought of getting out. He made a face and I knew he was going to shoot down my idea.

"You call that food?" He asked.

"Whatever" I got up from the floor and began pulling clothes out of my closet, trying to find something nice to wear to whatever fancy restaurant he had in mind. He followed behind me, wrapping his arms around my waist.

"I'm sorry, Sinthia." He apologized and kissed my cheek. "We can go to your burger joint, if that's what you want to do." I felt guilty for throwing a temper tantrum. I liked John, I really did, but sometimes he came across as being better than I am.

"It's fine. We can go wherever you want." I sighed heavily, tugging at a silk blouse in my closet. He turned me around and cupped my face in his hands.

"Come on. Let's go to Smokey's." He smiled, looking into my eyes. I leaned in to kiss him and he pecked me on the lips, pulling away quickly.

The parking lot at Smokey's was packed. We parked along the road and John complained the entire walk to the door about leaving his car out on the main street. I tried desperately not to roll my eyes at him. If I had a car as expensive as his, I would be worried about something happening to it too.

We sat in the far corner of the restaurant because John could not stand the smoke that lingered around the other tables. When the server arrived to take our orders John ordered us two sodas and a Stromboli, not giving me the chance to speak.

"Actually..." I spoke up and the server turned back around to face me. "I'll have a beer." She smiled and wrote down my drink order. I looked over at John who was making a face.

"That sounds fun. I will have a beer as well. What do you have that's imported?" he asked.

"Umm..." She looked at me for help.

"We will have two Buds." I chimed in and she walked away quickly.

"This should be fun." He said as he looked around the room. Just then, the door opened and Collin's green eyes locked on to mine. I sat up straighter, wishing I had listened to John about going somewhere else. He had a brunette under his arm and she placed her

hand on his chest. Taylor, Beef and Jake
followed behind.

"What is it?" John asked, reaching over
and placing his hand on mine. I pulled back,
putting my hands on my lap.

"Just some old friends of mine" He
followed my eyes and caught site of who I was
staring at.

"Quite a colorful past you have Sinthia."
He teased. I knew he was uncomfortable as he
stared at Collins tattoos. "Invite them to join
us." He said, smiling.

"No...no" I waved away the idea as the
server set our drinks in front of us. I grabbed my
beer and immediately drank half of it down in
one sip.

"Woah, Sinthia. You are never going to
be able to study tonight if you drink like that."
He pulled the beer from my hand. My cheeks
burned red and I glanced over to my old friends
who were talking quietly and glancing over in
my direction. Taylor sat her purse on the table
and walked in towards us.

"Sin, where the fuck have you been?" John nearly fell out of his chair at her language.

"Around" I replied, tucking my hair behind my ear. John cleared his throat.

"Taylor this is John. John this is my friend Taylor." Pleasure to meet you John said holding out his hand. Taylor looked at him sideways and took his hand to shake it.

"Umm...Sin, we were wondering if you would like to hit Filly's with us tonight. You know...catch up a little?" I looked over at John biting my lip. It had taken everything to get him to come here and I knew he would never do it again.

"Looks like Collin is doing good without his wingman." I said, glancing over at the brunette on his arm. He was whispering in her ear and she was giggling.

"Yea...She's been hanging around a lot." Her eyes looked down at her feet. My heart sank in my stomach.

"That's great." I lied.

"What the heck. Let's go out." John smiled. Taylor looked at me as if I was visiting from another planet.

"Great. I guess we will see you *both* around nine?"

"Sure" I sighed, smiling over at John. Taylor made her way back across the room as everyone stared at her expectantly. She told them the news and they all yelled and cheered, everyone except for Collin. He glanced my way then squeezed his date tighter to him.

I had practically emptied my closet on my bed. I could not find anything suitable to wear out drinking that John would approve of. It was times like these I really missed Taylor. I settled on an old pair of tight torn up jeans and a small t-shirt that hugged my body in all the right places.

"Well, this is fun." He said, eyeing up my outfit. "Perhaps I should change." He was wearing a button up shirt and khaki pants.

"You look great!" I leaned in to kiss him. He gave me his cheek.

Chapter Eight

Filly's was packed as usual and the crowd spilled out into the parking lot. John took the long way around them as we made our way to the front door.

"We can leave whenever you want." I assured him as I pulled open the door. The music pounded through my chest and I held John's hand as we made our way across the dance floor. Taylor and the guys were already at the bar doing a round of shots.

"Taylor" I yelled, tapping her on the shoulder. She spun around and wrapped her arms around my neck.

"It's been so long!"

"Let's get you a shot!" She smiled and I glanced back at John.

"I'm just going to go use the restroom." He leaned in and kissed me on the cheek before leaving. I turned back to Taylor who was looking at me through narrowed eyes.

"What?" I asked as she grabbed two shots from the bar and handed me one.

"What the fuck is with that guy?" She asked, slamming back her drink. I drank mine and it burned more than I remembered.

"He's a nice guy." I said flatly.

"Exactly!" She laughed and I smacked her playfully on the arm. A pair of large arms wrapped around my waist from behind and lifted me into the air in a bear hug.

"Sin!" Beef yelled and I squealed as he squeezed me tighter.

"Beef!" I giggled and he set me back down. I spun around and gave him a hug. Jake followed suit and hugged me. We all drank another shot as I looked around the room. "Where's Collin?" I asked.

"He's..." Beef began but Collin's face appeared behind him.

"I'm right here." He grinned. "Hey, Sin." He nodded. I looked beside him at the brunette that still clung to him. "This is Sam." He pulled her closer to his body.

"Nice to meet you." I smiled. "Another shot?" I asked and everyone erupted around me. We slammed back two as I finally saw John coming back across the floor. I realized I may have had a little too much too quickly. "John!" I exclaimed, wrapping my arms around his neck. He pushed me back, looking at my face in confusion.

"How much have you had already?" He asked. Beef walked up beside me and put his arm over my shoulder.

"She can handle it, trust me." He smiled.

"John this is Beef." I giggled at his name. Beef rolled his eyes and squeezed my neck slightly harder.

"I'm sorry, did you say…" john began. Beef stuck out his hand in front of him.

"Beef. It's a…family name." He glanced at me out of the corner of his eye and I laughed again. John took his hand.

"Enough of this. Let's dance!" Taylor called from behind me. Everyone headed over to the dance floor leaving John and I standing awkwardly alone. I gestured my head towards the dance floor but he politely declined.

"I think I'd like to sit down for a bit." He yelled in my ear over the music. I began to sit next to him on a bar stool but Taylor grabbed my arm.

"Oh, no you don't! I need a dance partner!" She smiled and pulled me away. I shrugged my shoulders at John and he nodded and smiled. We made our way through the crowd as a new song began. I shook my hips with her and it had felt just like old times. That was until I spotted Collin out of the corner of my eye. Sam had her hands wrapped around his neck and they grinded their hips together as the full on made out in the middle of the floor. Taylor caught me staring and grabbed my hand, twirling me around in front of her.

"He looks happy." I yelled in her ear. She shrugged and kept dancing.

"She's been around a lot lately." She yelled back in my ear.

"At the house?" I quit moving and was just waiting for answers. She nodded, gauging my reaction. "He never takes girls to the house." I frowned. She shrugged her shoulders and grabbed my waist, making me dance with her again.

"What's with that John guy?" She made a face and I could not help but laugh.

"He's a good guy." I shrugged.

"You said that already." I turned around and looked at John as he sat talking on his cell phone.

"I can trust him." I nodded. Jake moved up beside us, dancing along as we swayed our hips.

"What up Sin? Finally settle down?" He joked, nodding in John's direction. I smiled and nodded my head.

"He's a good guy." I yelled over the music. Jake made a sour face.

"Sounds boring!" I smacked his arm and rolled my eyes.

"Come on guys! I thought you wanted me to get with someone?" I looked back and forth between them and they just stared at each other.

"I'm going to get us some shots. You aren't laughing nearly hard enough at Beef." He smiled and made his way to the bar next to John. I could see them talking and I became worried he would make John feel out of place. Jake had always been overprotective of me like a brother.

After another song had finished Jake and Beef came over carrying shots for all of us. I glanced over at John who was busy typing away on his phone.

"He didn't want one. Fucking lightweight." Beef said, rolling his eyes. I smacked him on the arm causing some alcohol to spill out of one of the shots. "Woah! Party foul!" He teased. Collin walked up behind me and reached around my waist, grabbing a shot and slamming it back. He looked at me, his face inches from mine and I looked ahead. The smell of his soap took me back to the nights I used to cuddle with him in his bed. His hard chest rubbed against my back and I stiffened, not wanting to relax against him. I grabbed a shot from Beef's hands and slammed it back without blinking an eye.

"How have you been?" Collin's breath blew warmly against my neck.

"Good" I said quietly, biting my lip.

"Good" He replied and backed away from me. I let out a deep breath and turned around to face him.

"Where's Sam?" I asked, glancing around.

"She had to go home. Classes tomorrow" He explained. "I'm going to get another shot. You want one?" He asked, taking the shot glass from my hand. When his fingers brushed against mine, I could feel the electricity between us.

"Sure" I nodded and he headed over to the bar next to John. I watched them chat for a moment, wondering what Collin could possibly be saying to him.

"Why don't you guys just knock this shit off already? We miss hanging out with you,"

Taylor yelled in my ear. "It's obvious you guys fucking like each other." My cheeks burnt red.

"He doesn't fucking like me, Tay. He fucks everything that walks but when it came to me he couldn't even go through with it." I stared at her hard, wishing I had not brought up the past.

"He thinks you deserve better." She said seriously.

"That's ridiculous." I turned around to look over at Collin and John. Collin had his back against the bar and was looking in my direction. I smiled nervously and he grinned back.

"I'm surprised he hasn't tried to fight John to the death for you." Taylor laughed. I rolled my eyes at her.

"John's not that kind of guy."

"He wouldn't fight for you?" She asked and I did not have an answer. Collin patted John on the back and made his way back across the room.

"Here" he held out a shot for me and one for Taylor. "John said he needs to get home and study." I pouted, not ready to leave just yet. "I told him I would make sure you got home safe." He smiled in that devilish way that gave me butterflies. I shot him a dirty look as John walked over to us.

"I have to get some studying in before it gets too late." He frowned and I nodded. "Have fun with your friends. I'll see you tomorrow." He leaned in and kissed me on the cheek.

"Bye John." I smiled as he walked away.

"Bye John" My friends yelled and waved after him, making fun of me.

"He kisses you like you're his fucking Grandma, Sin. That's fucking hot." Collin laughed and I jammed my elbow into his ribs causing him to choke on his shot.

"Yes, make fun of him for not fucking everything that walks." I clenched my jaw before slamming back my drink.

"I don't fuck everything that walks!" Collin replied, insulted. I narrowed my eyes at him. He leaned in to speak directly into my ear. "I didn't fuck you." I felt all of the blood leave my face at the coldness of his words.

"Not like I would have let you!" I shot back. He grinned and I could tell he had drunk away his filter.

"Please. I could have had you the first night I brought you back to my place." His eyes were glazed and I could tell he must have started drinking long before they had gotten to the bar.

"Yea, well, you didn't and now that's John's job." My eyes burned into his and he looked livid. He moved his face practically against mine until we were breathing each other's air. He did not say anything. He pushed passed me and I let out the breath I had not realize I had been holding. I stood in the middle of the dance floor fighting back tears as I tried to figure out what had just happened.

"Are you okay?" Taylor asked, putting her hand on my shoulder. I bit my lip and shook my head no.

"I'll take you home." She said and I followed her out of the club. Collin sat on the curb just outside the front door and he jumped up when he saw me.

"Sin!" He called after me and I walked faster after Taylor. "Sin!" He grabbed my arm, spinning me around to face him.

"Oww!" I yelled, trying to pry his fingers off me.

"I didn't mean it." His eyes were sad and full of regret.

"Doesn't matter" I pulled at his fingers but he did not let up.

"Hey! Let's not do this here." Taylor stepped in between us, staring at Collin. He nodded and his hand slowly released me. I rubbed my arm.

"Can we talk?" He looked passed Taylor at me. A tear escaped my eye and I wiped it away quickly, hoping he had not noticed.

"Maybe some other time" I said, my voice shaking. He nodded but did not say anything else.

Taylor and I rode back to the dorms in silence. When we finally pulled up, she spoke.

"So...not exactly how I saw it going." She laughed nervously.

"Things are just too different now." I shrugged and she nodded in agreement. "I'll see you around." I smiled at her as I got out of the car.

"Yea" Her voice trailed off.

I could not wait to crawl under my covers. As soon as I made it inside my room, I slid down the door, pulling my knees tight against my chest and cried. I did not even know why. I knew now that I had made the right decision to stay away from Collin. He was too much of a wild card. I thought about what he had said and the words stung all over again. I was the one who had ruined our friendship. He never wanted anything more.

Chapter Nine

The next day I was late for my first class and had forgotten my notes. When class was over I walked towards the large glass doors and I could see Collin staring back at me. I took a deep breath and walked outside, continuing past him.

"You're up early." I said as he walked a step behind.

"Yea, I wanted to talk to you about last night." I turned to face him and he was running his hands though his hair.

"Don't. I do not know what I was thinking. I guess I had a little too much to drink." I replied, biting my lip.

"I shouldn't have said..." His voice trailed off and he took a step closer to me. I took a step back.

"Water under the bridge" I smiled. He nodded, searching me with his bright green eyes. John walked up behind me and placed his arm around my waist, oblivious to the tension in the air.

"Hey, Collin! Fun night last night." He grinned, looking back and forth between us.

"Yea. It was a real hoot." Collin replied and I choked on my own laughter at his words. He grinned out of the side of his mouth. "We were thinking of going out again tonight, if you're up for it?"

"Yea, sure." He wrapped his arm unnaturally around my neck. "My girl and I will be there." Collin glanced my way when John called me 'his girl'. "Got to get to class." John kissed me on the cheek and waved to Collin who nodded his head once.

"We're going out again?" My stomach was doing summersaults.

"Yea, why not? John seems like a nice guy." He stared at me, no expression on his face.

"Yea, he is." The silence between us grew awkward for a moment. "I should get going." He nodded again.

As soon as Collin had turned his back, I pulled out my cell phone and called Taylor.

"You're fucking kidding me. He invited you both out?" Taylor sounded as shocked as I was. "I'm not sure that's such a good idea." For once, she agreed with me. "I mean…John's kind of boring." I could not help but let my mouth fall open.

"He's not boring!" I argued but I understood what she meant. He was nothing like the rest of us. He liked to stay home, he did not get in trouble, and most of all he would never hurt me. She laughed into the receiver.

"Okay, Sin. I'll see you tonight."

"Whatever" I hung up the phone and stalked off to my room. I decided to skip the rest of my classes and focus on what I would wear for the night. After tearing all of the clothes from my closet, I could not find a single thing to wear. I cursed myself for leaving most of my 'clubbing' clothes at Collin's house. After hanging everything back up, I called a cab and made my way across town to find the perfect outfit. Shopping was one of my least favorite past times but I wanted to make sure everyone knew I still knew how to have fun. I tried on countless clothes in at least half a dozen stores before coming up with the perfect dress. A bright blue strapless dress that could barely be considered anything more than a shirt. I matched it with a new pair of black heels that I had found for half off.

I made it back to my dorm with enough time to shower and curl my hair so it hung in large soft layers around my face. I spent the little bit of time I had left doing my makeup and convincing myself that I could summon the courage to actually go out in public.

John knocked on the door a little while later. I pulled it open slowly, biting my lip as he took in my ensemble.

"Wow" he said with a nervous laugh.

"You like it?"

"Well...It is a little revealing." I tugged at the bottom of my skirt and frowned.

"It is a little short, but the color is really beautiful, don't you think?" He cleared his throat and thought of how to respond. "You don't like it?" I felt my heart sink. In a matter of seconds, I went from feeling like a princess to a piece of trash. I threw my little black clutch on my bed and stalked over to my closet. I began ripping out all of my clothing onto the floor below my feet.

"Sinthia, it is fine, really. I didn't mean to upset you." I rolled my eyes and continued digging. He was being too nice. It made the entire situation worse.

"If you don't like it than you don't like it. Don't say what you think I want to hear." I do not know why I was being so mean to him, but at that moment I could not stand how polite and calm he was when I was about to explode.

"Sin, stop." He placed his hand on my arm.

"Don't call me that." I whipped around, pulling back from his touch.

"What?" He looked genuinely offended and I immediately regretted what I had said. I wiped a stray tear from my cheek and took a deep breath.

"I just...I like it when you call me Sinthia."

Chapter 10

By the time we made it to the club, I had smoothed things over with John. I felt incredibly guilty for being so short with him and I was not even sure why I was so upset. I had wanted a conservative and trustworthy boyfriend and that was exactly who he was. I could not blame him for not wanting me out wearing next to nothing. I glanced down at my blue dress and back to him. I should have changed. I should have not made him agree to go out like this if he was uncomfortable and I had no idea why I felt so conflicted. We ordered a round of drinks and waited by the bar for everyone else to arrive.

"You want to dance?" I asked as 'Wild Ones' played over the speakers. He shook his head.

"You know I don't really like to dance." He was practically blushing as he glanced around at the couples grinding their hips into one another on the dance floor.

"I'll dance with you." Collin said into my ear from behind me. I turned around, nearly spilling my drink. "That is if you don't mind."

Collin was staring at John with a polite smile on his face.

"Sure, why not?" John replied, but I could tell he didn't really like the idea. I could not contain the ridiculous grin that spread across my face. Collin took my hand and pulled me through the sea of people as Taylor and the others circled around John, ordering a round of drinks.

Collin wrapped his hands around my waist, pulling my body flush against his. I stood frozen for a moment, worried that John might get upset.

"He's fine" Collin motioned towards John. He was busy downing a drink with the rest of the group and they were yelling and cheering as they ordered more. I relaxed and moved my hips to the music against Collin's. I slid my hands up his chest, coming to rest on the sides of his neck as his slid lower. "You look amazing tonight." He whispered in my ear as one of his hands brushed over my bottom, holding me firmly against him. The feel of his breath on my ear sent a shiver down my spine. Our cheeks were resting against each other's as we moved together to the music. I panted in his ear as we grinded together, completely oblivious to the world around us. The song ended and a new more upbeat one began. I pushed back from him slightly, but his hands clung tightly around my body.

"I should get back to John." I said, realizing how lost in the moment I had gotten.

"He's having fun. So are we." Collin smirked but I suddenly felt horribly guilty.

"Come on. Let's get a drink." I pushed back harder and he finally relaxed his grip, allowing me to step back. I tucked my hair behind my ear and made my way back to the bar. Collin's hand grabbed mine but I pulled away, not wanting to hold it.

"Hey! Where have you been?" John asked, his words slurring together. I looked at Taylor and the others. She was grinning guiltily and Beef just shrugged, taking a sip from his beer and refusing to look me in the eye.

"I was dancing, remember?" I explained, grabbing the beer from Beef and Taking a long drink, finishing it off.

"This isn't funny." I scolded Taylor.

"Come on. We're just having a little fun."

"A little? You practically gave him alcohol poisoning in a matter of minutes."

"Let's get another round for my friends here!" John yelled to the bartender who rolled her eyes as she filled the shot glasses.

"I think you had enough." I leaned in towards John and put my hand on his so he could not drink. He pulled back from me angrily.

"I have had enough, Sinthia." My name coming out long and drawn out.

"I think we should call it a night." I put my arm on his, hoping to calm him down. He grabbed his shot, slamming it back. He made a sour face for a moment than stood up from his bar stool. His eyes locked on to Collin's.

"You know, just because my girl is dressed like a slut doesn't mean she is going to sleep with you." He growled angrily and I felt my cheeks burn red. Collin put his hand up on John's chest, warning him to stop. "She doesn't sleep with anyone, do ya' Sinthia?"

"I'm fucking warning you." Collin's voice was low and steady. I knew it was only a matter of seconds before he lost control.

"No, I am warning you!" John poked his finger into Collin's chest. "I can see what you are trying to do. Sinthia is too good for you. You are nothing but trash." He hissed and I felt my blood begin to boil.

"That's enough!" I yelled at John. He had gone too far. His holier than thou attitude was really beginning to piss me off.

"Shut up, Slut." John slurred. As soon as the words left his mouth, Collin cocked back his fist, planting a blow across the side of John's face, sending him crashing against the bar.

"Stop it!" I screamed, trying desperately to pull Collin back from John. Beef pushed his way between us and Jake pulled me back, trying to calm me down.

"I think our friend here has had a little too much to drink. I'm going to make sure he gets home safely." Beef said, holding John by the collar of his shirt as blood trickled down his face. My head was spinning. I was angry at John for the things he had said, but mostly at what he had said to Collin. I was very overprotective of my friends. Honestly, I was mostly angry with myself. I should have said no to going out with Collin and I should have never stepped onto the dance floor with him, knowing how I felt.

"Come on. I'll take you home." Collin said, still trying to steady his breathing. He was angrier than I had ever seen him before, which was saying a lot. I nodded, hesitantly. I followed Collin out into the night air. The quiet and calm outside of the club was almost overwhelming. I slid into the seat and we rode in silence, not certain if I should thank him for defending my honor, or smack him for hitting my boyfriend. John had every right to be upset. I had made him feel uncomfortable from the beginning by wearing this ridiculous outfit. I tugged at the bottom of my shirt.

"You really do look amazing." Collin broke the silence, glancing at me out of the corner of his eye. I noticed we had driven passed my dorm.

"Where are we going? I thought you were taking me home?" I looked out the window as the building grew smaller.

"I didn't say *your* home." Collin grinned and pressed down on the gas pedal. I glared at him, but could not help but smile. I had missed spending time with him.

Chapter 11

When I stepped inside Collin's place, it felt like I had never left. He made his way into the kitchen and poured us a few drinks.

"I'm sorry about hitting John." He said as he poured another round.

"I can't say he didn't ask for it." I drank down the harsh shot. Collin ran his hands through his dark hair.

"He's not right for you. I mean...I know he's the kind of guy you think you need, but he isn't what you want." Collin rounded the counter and stood in front of me.

"How do you know what I want?" I asked, my voice shaking as I looked up into his bright green eyes. He stepped closer, his eyes burning into mine. I held my breath, unable to step away.

"I know I'm no good for you, Sin. I know you deserve better." He reached up, running his fingers along my jaw.

"Don't talk about yourself that way." I grabbed his hand, holding it in mine. "You're...amazing" My voice trailed off as the electricity flowed between us. My emotions were all over the place. I had convinced myself that Collin did not look at me as anything but a friend, that all of the flirting and sexual tension was a figment of my imagination. He leaned his face closer to mine, his warm breath blowing against my lips.

"I have wanted you from the moment I met you." Without thinking, I pushed my lips against his. He returned my kiss and we stood there with our lips pushed hard against each other's for what felt like a lifetime.

"Are you sure this is what you want?" His breath was erratic and I could tell he wanted this as badly as I did. I bit my lip and nodded and a small grin spread across his face. He kissed me again, this time parting my lips with his tongue. I pushed back with mine, mirroring his movements. He moaned quietly into my mouth. I had been in love with Collin from the very beginning. I thought I could fight it, that I needed something else, but in this moment, he we were the only people in existence.

We walked down the hallway to his room, our mouths never leaving each other. He closed the door behind us and wrapped his arms around me tightly, pulling me closer against him. I ran my fingers through his hair, not hiding how much I needed him.

"We can stop at any time." He reassured me.

"Don't stop," I moaned. He grabbed the bottom of my dress and pulled it up over my head, taking a moment to look at me, he pulled his shirt over him. I ran my fingers over his hard chest, as his muscled flexed beneath them. I trailed down his stomach to the waist of his jeans, looking back up at him. I unsnapped his button and slid his pants down to the floor. He pushed me back onto the bed, falling with me. His fingers laced in mine and he pushed them against the mattress as he kissed me harder than he had before. I pushed back against him, unable to get enough.

"What the hell are you doing?" Our bodies froze.

I glanced towards the doorway to see Sam blocking the entrance.

"Sam!" Collin yelled. I was completely mortified. She turned and headed down the hallway. He pushed off the bed quickly and pulled on his jeans, running after her. I lay there by myself for a moment unable to process what had just happened. I was going to leave my boyfriend for him and he was chasing after his girlfriend. I pushed back the lump in my throat and grabbed my clothing. I got dressed quickly and flew down the steps out of the apartment.

"Sin, wait!" Collin called after me, his girlfriend standing in front of him with her arms crossed over her chest. I could feel the tears about to fall and I started running down the block. I needed to get as far away from him as possible. I felt sick.

By the time I made it to my dorm, I looked like something that had crawled out of a gutter. My cheeks where smeared with mascara and my hair was wild and knotted. Luckily, the elevator was empty and I rode up to my room, quietly crying to myself. As I walked down the hall, I could see a figure sitting by my door. John was slumped, sleeping against the wall, his phone in his hand. I unlocked my room and slowly opened the door beside him, sliding inside. I did not want to speak to him after betraying him with Collin. Everything he had said tonight was right. I crawled into my bed and curled up in a ball, wishing I could disappear.

The next morning I awoke feeling worse than the night before. I sat alone in my room for hours listening to depressing music as my phone rang off the hook. John banged on my door for nearly an hour until he finally took the hint and left. I could not face him. He may have been what I thought I needed but he deserved so much better. After I was sure I was alone, I made my way down the hall to take a nice long hot shower. I could not get my mind off Collin. As hard as I tried to be just friends with him, my heart wanted more. I decided I needed to take some time away from this place and get my head straight. After my shower, I packed a bag of belongings and called my mother. I told I was homesick and needed a break from my work. She ordered me a ticket online for later that night. I only had a few more hours of avoiding everyone before I could finally get away. I made myself something to eat and sat in the dark, replaying last night over and over in my head. A knock came at the door and I sat quiet, afraid to breathe.

"Sin?" Taylor called. "I know you're in there. I just want to talk." I reluctantly unlocked the door. "You look like shit." She said as she slid passed me. I locked the door behind her.

"Thanks" I rolled my eyes and plopped back down on my bed.

"Collin..."

"Don't!" I cut her off, glaring at her. She put up her hands.

"Fair enough." She sighed and we sat in silence for a few minutes as I ate my soup. "What's with the bag?" She nodded to my luggage at the foot of my bed.

"I'm going home for a few days." I said, not meeting her stare.

"Sin, you can't just leave!"

"I can. I am. Plane leaves at six." I replied, taking another bite.

"Collin is going insane!" She explained.

"I guess juggling a bunch of women will do that to you." I rolled my eyes and she sighed dramatically.

"He's not *juggling* anyone. He has not been the same since you stopped coming around. He finally began seeing Sam after we all convinced him it would help him take his mind off of you." She said, exasperated. I glanced up with her, not believing what she was saying. "He avoids her at all cost."

"He certainly didn't avoid her last night."

"Put yourself in his position. He could not just let her leave like that. He went to explain to her that he loved you." Her words shot through me like a dagger.

"He what?"

"It's obvious, Sin. He never wanted to make a move because he thought you deserved better than him." I shook my head. I hated that he thought he was not good enough for me. "He's dying right now because he thinks he has lost you forever." My heart sank. I never thought in a million years that he was hurting as much as I was. "Can you please just talk to him?"

"I can't." I wiped a wayward tear from my cheek and she nodded.

"Just...call me if you need anything." She said and walked over to my door, sliding out and closing it behind her. I cried for a few more minutes deciding what to do. It was obvious I was making a mess of the lives around me and I needed to set things straight. I scrolled through my phone, taking a deep breath before dialing.

'Sinthia?" John asked, relieved I had finally called him back.

"John, we need to talk." I said, waiting for his response.

"I'll be right over." I glanced down at my luggage.

"No. I'll meet you outside."

"Fair enough"

I sat out front on the curb of the dorm waiting for John to arrive. My heart was racing a mile a minute as I tried to figure out what I was going to say to him. When he arrived, I thought about running back into the building but when I saw his face, I could not move. His eye was an unnatural shade of purple and his cheek was swollen to twice its normal size.

"Oh my God!" I called out, pushing to my feet. He put up his hands to wave off my worry.

"I deserved it. I shouldn't have said all those things last night."

"I understand why you did." He smiled a little and my stomach turned. "We need to talk." I was ringing my hands together out of nervousness. "I like you, I really do, but I don't think we are right for each other."

"What? Sinthia, we are perfect for each other."

"No, I tried to be what you wanted but it's not fair to either one of us." He stepped forward but I put up my hand to stop him.

"So that's it?" he asked, sounding defeated. I nodded and he shook his head.

"I'm sorry," I said and he looked down at the ground, kicking a few stones.

"Don't be. Have a good life, Sinthia." He turned and made his way back to his car. I took a deep breath and went back into the dorm. I felt a lot better about everything going on but I still had not figured things out with Collin. I grabbed my luggage and called the local cab company. My phone rang off the hook as I sat on the curb waiting for my ride. Collin's voicemails ranged from sad to downright pissed off. I turned the sound off as the cab pulled up. A million thoughts ran through my head as we reached our destination. I paid the driver and watched him drive down the road and disappear. I turned to look at Collin's building, summoning the courage to go inside.

Chapter Twelve

"Sin!" Collin yelled from his window. I shielded my eyes from the sun to look up at him.

"I'll be right down!" He yelled and in record time, he burst through the front door of the building. He walked slowly towards me as if I were a mirage that would disappear at any second. "I thought you were going home?" He asked looking confused and relieved at the same time.

"I'm here aren't I?" I smiled. He laughed and took a step closer to me.

"Kiss her you idiot!" Taylor yelled from the window above us. We glanced up to see Taylor, Beef and Jake staring at us like a sideshow.

Collin wrapped his arms around my waist and pulled me hard against him, his lips finding mine hungrily. Cheering erupted from above us as my feet left the ground. He slid his hand under my knees and carried me in up the front steps.

"Make yourself useful and come grab her things!" Collin yelled up at the window. He carried me effortlessly up the steps as Beef slid by us to retrieve my belongings.

"Thanks Beef!" I smiled. He turned back at me and winked. Collin kissed me quickly on the cheek as he kicked open the front door. Taylor and Jake stood on the other side clapping and cheering. "I feel like I'm in a John Hughes movie." I laughed as Collin set me down.

"This is your kingdom. Everything the light touches..." Collin began in a deep voice.

"Lion King? Really?" I punched him in the arm.

"Ouch! You hit almost as hard as I do!" He yelped.

"You guys are meant for each other!" Taylor rolled her eyes. "Where are we going to celebrate?" She looked at us expectantly.

"I don't know about you lightweights but I could use a beer." I smiled. Collin picked me up and swung me around.

"First, I get to do something I have been dreaming of for months. Body shots!" Collin yelled.

"I got this." Beef picked me up like a sack of potatoes and threw my over his shoulder. I kicked and screamed as he sat my on the kitchen counter. I laughed and screamed as they held me down and Collin poured tequila into my belly button and slurped it out. It tickled and I fought against them to let me go.

"Alright. I think she has been tortured enough. Let's go party!" Taylor yelled. I crawled off the counter and jumped Collin's back. He carried me down the steps and we headed to Filly's for 'Midnight Margarita' night.

The place was pack, as usual and we had to fight our way up to the bar. We each got our margaritas and headed out onto the dance floor. 'If' began bumping through the speakers and I used it to my advantage. I shook my hips against Collin. I spun around and dropped my hands to the floor. I flipped my hair back as I slowly stood up against him, reaching behind me and running my hands down his neck.

"Shit, Sin. Where did you learn to dance like that?" His hands slid down my sides.

"Television, duh." I laughed. He turned me around, pulling me tight against him.

"You have no idea how many times I wanted to do this." He leaned in and kissed me in the middle of the dance floor. Our friends around us yelled and clapped like a bunch of drunken fools and I loved every minute of it. I felt like I was in the middle of a sappy love story that just kept getting better.

"Take me to bed or lose me forever!" I said dramatically, channeling Meg Ryan in Top Gun. I found it fitting after being called 'wingman' for the past several months.

"You don't have to ask me twice." Collin lifted me in his arms and the crowd parted around us as we made our way to the door.

When we reached the apartment, I could barely think straight. I had thought about this moment for months but now that it had arrived, I suddenly felt afraid.

"We don't have to do this now. We have forever." Collin reassured me, tucking my hair behind my ear.

"Shut up and take me to bed already!" I grabbed his face in my hands and pulled his mouth to mine. He kissed me back, as we stumbled down the hallway together, unable to take our hands off each other. We reached his bedroom and he kicked the door shut behind us, turning the lock on the door.

"I should have done that the first time." He laughed. I smiled, pulling off my clothing as his face turned serious. "I love you, Sin." He breathed as he pulled off his shirt and grabbed my face again for another kiss. We collapsed in each other's arms onto the bed, tangled together.

"Collin..." I whispered. His expression looked worried as if he may have gone too far. "I love you." It felt like a huge weight lifting off me as the words left my mouth. I never meant anything more than those three tiny words. They carried the power of the world.

Five Years Later…

I unlocked the door to my home. It was small but it had a decent size backyard and was just minutes from downtown Savannah. The weather was always warm and the people were incredibly friendly. The house was dark as I slipped inside. Collin was working late tonight. I pushed the door open, my hands full of a few items I had picked up at the bakery. As I flicked on the lights, the room filled with sound.

"Surprise!" Everyone I loved in the world was there. Taylor ran up to hug me, leaning over my giant stomach. My Mom followed kissing me on the cheek. Tears sprung to my eyes.

"I thought you wouldn't be here until next month!" I wrapped my arms around my Mother's neck, squeezing her tightly.

"I couldn't miss your baby shower!" She replied, grabbing my face with her hands. "How is my grandson?" She placed her hand on my belly. I placed mine on hers and smiled. My eyes scanned the room, full of all of my friends. In the back, I spotted Collin, grinning. People

swarmed me and I could not take my eyes off
him.

The Con

Sneak Peek

Chapter One

"Honey, you're going to be late!" Ally called up the stairs to her husband, Anthony. They had been married for nearly eight years and without her, he would forget his own name. Moments later Anthony lumbered down the staircase, buttoning his shirt along the way. He smirked and grabbed his dark grey suit jacket from Alley, shrugging it on as he made his way out of the front door. Several seconds passed and the front door flew back open as Anthony returned for his keys that Ally held out in her hand with a smirk.

"Thanks, Hon." Anthony said and quickly pecked Ally on the cheek. She smiled as she walked into the kitchen, fixing her long dirty blonde hair into a loose bun, securing it with a pen she grabbed of off the counter top. She chewed her lip as she read over her schedule for the day. Her heart sunk as she read *Sadie's Fundraiser 3pm* scrawled out in the calendar block. She grabbed the island countertop with both hands to steady herself, closing her eyes and counting to ten. Tears stung her eyes as she squeezed them tighter begging them not to fall.

Her breathing became more rapid and uncontrolled. She reached for her purse and desperately searched for an orange pill bottle labeled valium. Panic set in as she knocked the purse to the floor and its contents scattered.

"Shit!" she muttered aloud as the flood gates opened and tears streamed down her face, stinging her cheeks. She collapsed to the floor and rummaged through the mess, coming up with her prescription bottle. She struggled desperately to pop the child safety cap off. The irony of not having a child to protect did not miss her. Her home was now sickeningly silent since she closed down her day care. Finally, the lid sprung free sending pills all over her lap. She gathered two and grabbed her glass of off the counter, filling it quickly with the water tap on the door of the stainless steel fridge. Swallowing the pills she took a moment to calm herself before finding her cell phone from the mess on the floor. She opened the address book and paused at her husband's name. After a moment, she continued down the list and selected the name Doctor Hemler. After three excruciatingly long rings, a receptionist answered the phone.

"Dr. Hemler's office. How may I help you?" a sweet soothing voice called through the receiver.

"Yes, um- is Doctor Hemler available?" Ally asked trying to keep the shaking in her voice hidden.

"He's in an appointment this morning. May I take a message and have him call you back?" The voice responded.

"NO-no." Ally stuttered and suddenly felt embarrassed by her breakdown. "I just forgot my appointment time, but I found the slip right here. My mistake." She said with a laugh. She clicked the end call button before the woman could respond. Taking a deep breath and finally feeling the effects from her medication Ally bend down to retrieve the contents of her purse. She quickly stuffed all of her belongings into her designer bag, hanging onto a picture of her beloved Sadie wearing a pink tutu.

Sadie was the spitting image of Ally, with long dirty blonde hair, big bright blue eyes and dimples framing her smile. She could have easily passed for her daughter. At four years old she dreamed of being a prima ballerina, taking lessons once a week at the Tutu Studio. Ally babysat her nearly every night, indulged in her every whim. They were partners and crime. Ally came alive when she was with Sadie. It was the only time her smile touched her eyes. One night in June while Sadie's parents were out of town for a business trip, they were leaving a local park after ditching pre-kindergarten to have ice cream and some good old-fashioned fun. They spent nearly two hours climbing trees and swinging from monkey bars.

"I think we better be getting home." Ally told Sadie as she checked her watch and realized Anthony would be home from work soon and she hadn't decided on anything for dinner.

"Awww." Sadie whined and gave her best pout trying to win a few extra moments of play time out of Ally.

"One more trip down the slide then we HAVE to go. You know how your Uncle Anthony gets when he is hungry." She said making an exaggerated angry face. Sadie giggled and ran off to the sliding board. She smiled and chatted with a little boy who had made it to the ladder just before her. Brushing the long blonde curls from her face she hurried up behind him, anxious to take her turn. Ally rummaged through her purse and checked her cell phone for messages. There were none, so she scrolled to her husband's name and sent him a quick text letting him know they would be home soon. As she hit send the horrible screeching of tires and metal colliding with something suddenly grabbed her attention. Time slowed as she whipped her head around to see what had made that awful noise. A crowd gathered around as the white car flipped into reverse and sped off, dragging its bumper under the front of it, sending sparks cascading down the road behind it. She quickly scanned the playground for Sadie. A little brown haired boy slid down and no one else was in sight. Her eyes darted to the swings that swayed empty. Her heart leapt into her throat as she searched desperately for the little girl.

"Sadie!" she panicked, her voice cracking and barely making a sound. "Sadie!" she called again, this time in a scream. She rushed to the crowd of onlookers, pushing through the crowd desperate to find her.

Ally's hands were still shaking as her tears fell onto the photo of the young girl. She stroked the picture with her thumb and she fought to swallow the lump in her throat. She had worked for two years to set up this charity event to help injured children in the name of Sadie, but she wasn't sure she was strong enough to go through with it. She smoothed out the corners of the picture and slid it back into her brown leather wallet. If she could get through that day she knew she could get through anything. She needed to do this for Sadie. She climbed the spiral stairs to her bedroom on the second floor. .The walls where covered in a soft ivory paper and the windows where adorned with intricately hand sewn lace curtains that her mother had given her as a house warming present. The sun shining through the windows sent wild patterns over the plain white comforter on the bed, making it look much more ornate than it actually was. Ally slid off her flesh colored heels and lumbered into the master bathroom to fix her make up before going to run errands. She flinched as she caught sight of her mascara that had run clear down to her chin. Without make up Ally could have easily been a model. She was a natural beauty that everyone envied but she never noticed. She had always felt awkward and outcast. Her father was a soldier in the army until she reached middle school when he was forced to retire after his arthritis in his knees became too much to bear. He was lucky enough to get an entry-level job at a new up and coming business. He worked hard and one promotion came after another until he had reached the top and the company exploded with success. With lots of hard work he managed to gain a small fortune that he quickly invested and nearly tripled his money. In high school, everyone envied her family's success. She was ridiculed and picked on until one day her mother had to pull her out and get her a tutor. She spiraled into a deep depression. She struggled to earn her diploma. When the day finally came, she had turned herself around enough to be excepted into a small but highly regarded college on the east coast. She could not wait to leave her life behind and start her own, being whoever she chose. Just two years into college, she had gone out drinking with a few friends at a local bar. A fight broke out between rival football players and Ally was left at the table alone to fend for herself as her friends scattered. As glass rained down from the wall behind her another student from the rival school grabbed her arm and pulled her out of the booth, shielding her from any harm. He had dark hair that was cut short, making him look much older than he was. When they reached the street he shrugged off his letterman jacket and slung it over Ally's shoulders. That was how she had met her husband. In six months time he had proposed. To avoid any backlash Ally and Anthony eloped, and she dropped out of college to set up a home for them and begin a daycare, her life-long dream. Anthony was a senior and was able to stick it out and graduate with his class. Ally's father welcomed Anthony into the family and his business. Anthony always promised to one day pay him back but that day seemed to get pushed further and further away.

The phone rang from the bedroom night stand as Ally was wiping the stains from her face, causing her to jump and poke herself in the eye. "Shit." She cursed herself and hurried over to the phone.

"Christiansen residence." She answered.

"Where the hell have you been? I thought something happened. Why haven't you answered your phone?" Anthony asked angrily. Ally rubbed her forehead hard.

"I must have left it downstairs. Everything okay?" she asked, not wanting to explain any further. He sighed and the line hung silent for a moment. Their relationship was strained, to say the least, when Ally could not move past the accident. She often wondered if they would have ever stayed together at all had it not been for the tragedy.

"Don't you have a busy day?" he asked and she knew he meant Sadie's fundraiser.

"Yea, I was just getting ready." She replied, letting her voice trail off.

"Better get a move on then." He said, not unkindly. She nodded but did not respond. After a moment, she heard his end of the line go dead and she hung up the phone. "Love you." She said quietly under her breath and headed back into the bathroom to finish getting ready for the day.

Available soon!

1112923R00068

Made in the USA
San Bernardino, CA
17 November 2012